Madeline Finn
and the
Therapy Dog

For the therapy dogs at my Quakertown Library. You and your
guardians continue to inspire me. And, for Sandy, the golden retriever
who brought so much love into the world.

—L. P.

Published by
Peachtree Publishing Company Inc.
1700 Chattahoochee Avenue
Atlanta, Georgia 30318-2112
www.peachtree-online.com

Text and illustrations © 2020 by Lisa Papp

Edited by Kathy Landwehr
Design and composition by Lisa Papp and Adela Pons

The illustrations were rendered in pencil and paper, with watercolor
and digital coloring.

Printed in December 2019 by Tien Wah Press in Malaysia
10 9 8 7 6 5 4 3 2 1
First Edition
ISBN 978-1-68263-149-2

Cataloging-in-Publication Data is available from the Library of Congress.

Madeline Finn
and the
Therapy Dog

Lisa Papp

PEACHTREE
ATLANTA

"Happy Birthday, Star!"

"Is Star ready for his test
tomorrow?" Mom asks.

"He sure is," I say.
"We've been practicing."

We practice meeting people.

"Hello, Madeline Finn," the postman says.

We practice sitting still when a bike goes by.

We even practice meeting other dogs.

"You're going to do great," I tell Star.

"You're going to make the best therapy dog ever."

Star doesn't go to a school for his test. Instead, we drive to a place called Walker Oaks.

"Star will have three visits here," Mom says.

"You can do it, Star," I say. "Remember, it's your job to make people smile."

Mrs. Dimple and Bonnie are waiting for us.

"Is this where Bonnie passed her therapy dog test?" I ask Mrs. Dimple.

"It sure is," she says. "Lots of therapy dogs visit the people who live here. If Star passes his test, he can join them."

Inside, we see a man with a clipboard.

"Hello, Madeline Finn," he says. "My name is Mr. Finch. It's my job to see if Star will make a good therapy dog."

"We've been practicing," I say.

"Would you like to hold Star's leash with your mother?" he asks.

"Yes, please," I say.

First Mom and I walk Star around the room.

"Stop please," Mr. Finch says. We stop.

"Proceed," he says. I guess that means "go," because
Mom starts walking again.

We walk past Bonnie and some other therapy
dogs. Star doesn't bark, or try
to play with them.

"Good job, Star," I say.

Next, Mr. Finch pets Star, especially touching his ears and tail.

Star doesn't mind.

A nurse walks past with a wheelchair.

Star is curious, but he doesn't chase it.

Finally, Mom and I have to let go of Star's leash and walk away.

Star is supposed to sit still.

But he doesn't…

Instead, he walks across the room. A lady smiles and Star puts his paw on her knee.

Mr. Finch writes something on his clipboard, but he's smiling too. "Okay," he says, "that's all for today."

"Star did well on his first test," Mom says when we leave.

"He sure did," Mrs. Dimple says. "On his next test, Star will visit with some of the residents."

"You can do it, Star," I say.

Star and I practice all week, especially sitting

still when I let go of his leash.

Pretty soon, it's time for his second test.

"Welcome back, Madeline Finn," Mr. Finch says.

This time, he leads us to a big room. "Why don't you and Star go in and say hello."

I'm kind of nervous, but Star isn't. He walks right up and smiles.

"Oh, isn't he the sweetest thing," a lady says.

"He reminds me of a dog I had when I was a boy," a man says.
He gives Star a kiss, right on his nose.

A lady with a big hat talks about her garden. She even reads Star
a letter. Star is a good listener.

Everyone seems happy.

Everyone except a man in

the corner.

"This is Mr. Humphrey," a nurse says.

"Would you like to pet Star?" I ask.

Mr. Humphrey doesn't say anything.

Mr. Finch takes some more notes.

Then it's time to go.

"Star did well on his second test," Mom says.

"But he didn't make Mr. Humphrey smile," I say.

"Some people need time," Mom says. "Remember how patient Bonnie was with you when you were learning to read?"

I think about that all the way home.

"You made a lot of people smile today," I tell Star when we get home. "We have to work on Mr. Humphrey though."

"Maybe he likes hide-and-seek. That might make him smile."

"Or card tricks."

"I don't think we can bring tennis
balls. Besides, Mr. Humphrey
might not have a mitt."

Before bed, Star and I practice reading together.

"You've got one more test," I say.

Then I tuck a few books into my bag.

Next time we visit Walker Oaks, Mr. Finch is waiting in the hallway. "Hello again, Madeline Finn," he says. "Today Star is going to ride the elevator."

"Oh no," I whisper. "We didn't practice that."

Star is afraid to go in. Then Bonnie gives him a little nudge.

The elevator is hot. And jiggly. And crowded.

"You can do it, Star," I say.

Finally, the door opens.

The hallway is busy.

Someone drops a plate of cookies, but Star leaves them alone.

Mr. Finch writes something on his clipboard.

"Good job, Star," I say.

Then we see Mr. Humphrey.

"This is Star," I say in my most patient voice.
"He's practicing to be a therapy dog. Would you like
to pet him?"

Mr. Humphrey doesn't say anything.

Maybe he doesn't hear me.

"Would you like to see my magic cards?" I ask after a while.

Still nothing.

Then Mrs. Dimple calls me over.

"Madeline Finn" she says, "do you remember when you first met Bonnie?"

I nod. "Bonnie liked me right away, even though I was afraid to read."

"That's right," Mrs. Dimple says. "Bonnie accepted you just as you are."

I look at Star. "Maybe Mr. Humphrey isn't ready to smile," I say. "Maybe we need to be patient."

"Mr. Finch, can we go back in?"

This time I sit by Mr. Humphrey but I don't say anything.

I just let him be.

After a while, I pull out my book. "I didn't always like to read,"
I whisper. "Especially out loud."

Mr. Humphrey doesn't say anything, but I don't mind.

When Bonnie sees me with a book, she comes right over.

I read nice and soft. I even mess up on a few words, but that's okay.

I'm almost to the end of my story when I see Star move closer
to Mr. Humphrey.

Very, very slowly, Star rests his chin on Mr. Humphrey's knee.

Finally, Mr. Humphrey looks at me. "My wife loved books," he says. And then he smiles. "How about another story?"

"Yes, sir," I say.

I'm picking out another book when Mr. Finch hands me something.

It's a tag for Star. I AM A THERAPY DOG, it says.

"You did it, Star!" And I fasten his new tag onto his collar,

right above his heart.